For Helen Gall
W.M.

For Jude
P.V.

Text copyright © 1986 by William Mayne
Illustrations copyright © 1986 by Peter Visscher
All rights reserved including the right of reproduction in whole or in part in any form.

Published in Great Britain by Walker Books Limited
Published by Prentice-Hall Books for Young Readers, A Division of Simon & Schuster, Inc.
1230 Avenue of the Americas, New York, NY 10020

10 9 8 7 6 5 4 3 2 1

Prentice-Hall Books for Young Readers is a trademark of Simon & Schuster, Inc.
Printed in Italy

Library of Congress Cataloging-in-Publication Data
Mayne, William, 1928–
Corbie.
Summary: Shunned by the other crows for his white feathers,
Corbie dreams of a better life and is generous to all.
[1. Crows—Fiction] I. Visscher, Peter, ill. II. Title.
PZ7.M4736Cr 1986   [E]   86-16991
ISBN 0-13-172602-1

CORBIE

Written by
William Mayne

Illustrated by
Peter Visscher

Prentice-Hall Books for Young Readers
A Division of Simon & Schuster, Inc.
New York

In a nest on the low branch
of a great tree in a courtyard
a baby bird grew his feathers.
"You are a crow, a crow," said his mother.
"Corbie is your name." And off she would
fly, black against the sky.

When she went Corbie's father came with a
crust, an egg, or tender meat. "You are a crow,"
he sang as he came down the wind. "A crow."

Corbie did not know one from another.
All crows are black, alike, and
careful of their young.

"Quiet there," called the oldest crow, on the top branch. At night the older crows talked wisely, high in the tree.

"One night we shall speak there," said Corbie's father. "We are too young now."

"We are not noticed at all," said his mother. "I wish we were."

All three were talked about when Corbie's feathers grew. Corbie was too young to know what he did wrong, but all the others saw.

They saw his feathers growing white instead of black.

"To think," said the older crows, "it's one of us, and what a vulgar color. It doesn't look quite dressed, and of course it'll never fly and that'll be the end of that."

"The cat will get it," said the oldest crow. "Let's talk of other things."

But Corbie grew, and Corbie flew. When he could find his own food, his parents left for town, to live in a tower and forget the past. All crows are strangers to their parents when they are grown.

The summer ended and the autumn came; then the winter long and cold. Corbie flew white against the dark sky.

In the spring the snow melted. Corbie
began to look for a wife, like all the rest. But
among the growing leaves he was alone. Girl
crows seemed not to see him; no one said a
word. His nest was empty, he had no wife,
no eggs, no one to feed. If he went visiting
he was severely pecked.

"Never mind," he said, "I'll see the world."

"The cat will get him," said the oldest crow,
raising his twentieth brood, all black.

But the cat that day took a starling that came to the ground for a red cheese rind.

"Where is my husband?" said the starling's wife. "Where has he gone? How shall I feed my children, all those mouths?"

Corbie picked up the rind of cheese. "The cat took him, I'm sorry to say," he said. "But here's what he was bringing home."

"Just like him to try something too large, the brave, stupid thing," said Mrs. Starling. "Up on the roof, please, in a hole in the chimney side. I won't stop to thank you: they'll want more in a minute and I'll have to find it. Just push it down their throats."

Off she went, so busy. Corbie put cheese rind down little throats, and no one pecked him.

"All the same," he said, "this sort of thing takes a lot of time, and I want to see the world." But he could not stop helping, and when the rind had gone he went to seek the cheese itself. "One more beakful each," he said. "But then I'm off to see the world."

"Kind of you," said Mrs. Starling, with her beak full.

"Just once more," said Corbie. "Then I'm definitely off."

"I think the cat got him," said the oldest crow. "He's not in the tree any more."

Corbie made his trip and set out to see the world. But he got no farther than the sausage maker, and flew back with one to feed the gaping mouths.

Corbie set off for the world, and came back with a beakful of caterpillars.

Corbie flew straight off, and came back at once with an unattended pie.

Corbie could not leave. He stayed, and taught the little ones to fly. And when they knew how, they flew away, and did not thank him or say goodbye.

"They've no manners," said their mother.
"They hardly knew their father,
  the fearless, feckless thing."

The summer went, the autumn went, the winter came. Corbie stayed at home, in the great tree in the courtyard where he was born.

"It's a patient cat," said the oldest crow.

Springtime came. Feathers fell from crows, and they flew about in rags while new ones grew. Corbie saw his feathers fall like snow.

When he felt neat again he went to find his friend on the roof.

"We did well last year," he said to Mrs.
Starling, "when you sadly lost your husband.
I don't have much luck among the crows.
I wonder if you'd marry me? There's a
rook along the roof who'd sign the book
and make it right."

"Oh, my dear," said Mrs. Starling, "I know
who you are. Yes, you did a kindly turn last
year; but don't you know? A starling cannot
marry with a crow, nor a crow with any
starling; besides, you're much too late, I've
been proposed to by such a darling.
You'd better stay in your tree."

So that was that. "No one wants me,"
said Corbie. "I'll see the world at once."
And he went back to the tree to say goodbye
to home and shed a little crowlike tear.

"Cat must have got him," said the oldest crow.
"I don't see him. My sight's not what it was."

On his branch, by his unmade nest, Corbie was about to fly. No one wants a white crow.

Someone touched him on the shoulder, a very little peck.

It was not the cat. It was a girl crow, looking at him so pretty and shy, her beak held down.

"Am I in your way?" asked Corbie. "I'll go at once."

"Where are your manners, crow?" she asked. "I'm looking for a husband. Don't you think I'm very nice?"

"Please don't tease me," said Corbie. "No one wants to marry a white crow."

"A white crow?" said the dark lady. "Are you color-blind or something?"

"No," said Corbie, and he stretched out his wing to show her. And when he looked he felt stupid and not at all brave. His new feathers were not white, but black, jet black, crow black. And he had not cared, or seen.

Now he saw that he was truly black
he flew off at once to bring her a present,
some noodles from the kitchen
of the house.

When he brought it to the tree the
girl crow was tidying the nest.
She knew he had said yes.

"We shan't live down here," said Corbie.
"I've been here long enough."

And off they went, to another tree of
their own, far off. Before they left they flew
up to say a polite Goodbye to the oldest
crow, although he had been unkind.

"Hello, young man," said the oldest crow. "Have you any news from down there? What happened to that white crow? Cat got him, did it?"

"I never saw him," said Corbie, and it was true. "Meet the wife. What did you say your name was, dear?"

"Corbelle," she said. And for Corbie all crows were black alike, except for her, and she was the coal-black beauty of them all. In the far-off tree she laid six whitey-greeny speckly eggs, and she and Corbie spent day and night warming them.

When they hatched he taught them to fly in black. When they had gone he and Corbelle set off for distant places, though they are all the world for each other now.

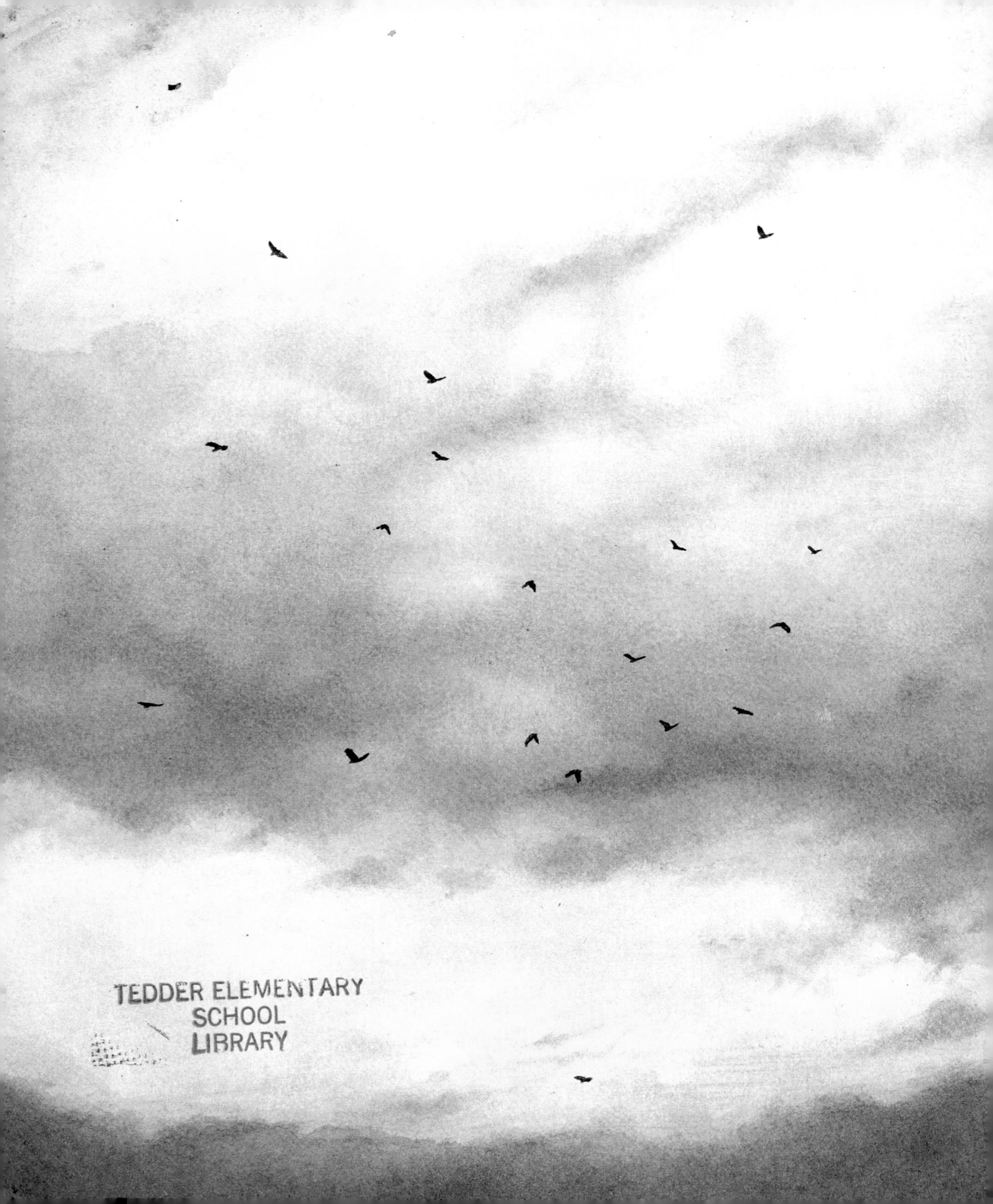